Other Books by Patricia Reilly Giff:

Matthew Jackson Meets the Wall
Illustrated by Blanche Sims

The Gift of the Pirate Queen
Illustrated by Jenny Rutherford

Casey, Tracy, and Company
Illustrated by Leslie Morrill
Poopsie Pomerantz, Pick Up Your Feet
Love, from the Fifth-Grade Celebrity
Fourth-Grade Celebrity
The Girl Who Knew It All
Left-Handed Shortstop
The Winter Worm Business
Rat Teeth

The Abby Jones, Junior Detective, Mysteries
Illustrated by Anthony Kramer
Have You Seen Hyacinth Macaw?
Loretta P. Sweeny, Where Are You?
Tootsie Tanner, Why Don't You Talk?

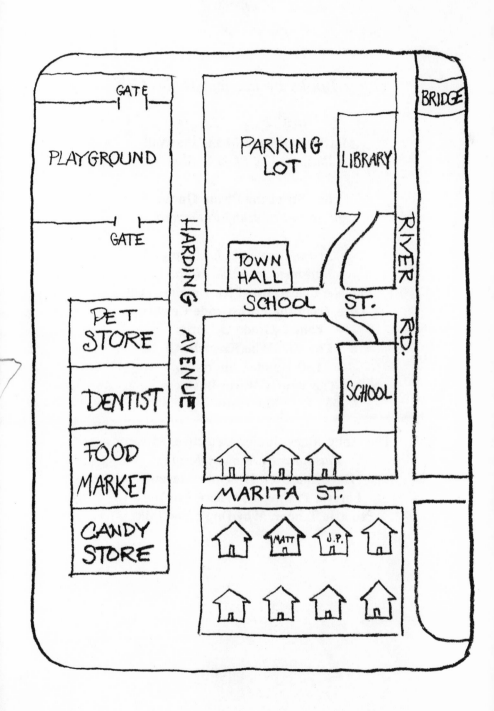

Shark in School

by Patricia Reilly Giff

Illustrated by Blanche Sims

Delacorte  Press

ACKNOWLEDGMENTS

*Special thanks to Jeanette Boehning and Jonathon Wilkinson
and the kids at Watervliet Elementary School.*

Published by
Delacorte Press
Bantam Doubleday Dell Publishing Group, Inc.
1540 Broadway
New York, New York 10036

Text copyright © 1994 by Patricia Reilly Giff
Illustrations copyright © 1994 by Blanche Sims

Library of Congress Cataloging in Publication Data

Giff, Patricia Reilly.
    Shark in school / by Patricia Reilly Giff.
        p.   cm.
    Summary: When Matthew finds out from J.P., the weird girl next
door, that their teacher loves to read, he worries that everyone at his
new school will know he's a terrible reader.
    ISBN 0-385-32029-9
    [1. Reading—Fiction. 2. Teacher-student relationships—Fiction.
3. Schools—Fiction. 4. Friendship—Fiction.]   I. Title.
PZ7.G3626Sh   1994
[Fic]—dc20   93-39016 CIP AC

Manufactured in the United States of America

September 1994

10 9 8 7 6 5 4 3 2 1

BVG

In Memory of William Clark . . .
Dear Bill

1

It was going to be a hot day. Matthew Jackson didn't have to open his eyes to know that.

He could feel the sun on his eyelids, warm and syrupy. His head was damp with the heat of it, his neck was sticky.

Barney, his cat, was a hot purring ball at his feet.

Good. He loved hot days. Swimming days. Do-nothing days.

He snapped his fingers at Barney. "Time to get up."

Barney stretched out one leg, then curled it underneath her again. She liked to sleep late.

Matthew sat up and leaned against the back of the bed. His room was at the top of the house. It was the attic, with a high pointy ceiling. The walls were painted blue, shiny and strong. He had picked the color out himself.

On the other side of the room he could see a wavery line, thick and red, painted on the wall. It stretched up from as far as two-year-old Laurie could reach, down to the molding on the floor.

"Good, Maffoo?" She had smiled, shaking her head hard. "Nice?"

"You drew a one," he had told her, not minding at all. It did look like a 1.

Last week he had told her she was Number 1.

Yesterday it reminded him of the one dollar he had found in front of the candy store.

Today it reminded him of something else.

Something terrible.

It meant only one day until school began.

He felt a quick flutter in his chest. Tomorrow he'd walk down the street to the River Road School. The school was long and low, and didn't

2

look anything like his old Polk Street School with its tall columns and high trees. And the only kid he'd know in his new class was J. P. Peterson, the girl next door.

He and J.P. were going to play golf in her backyard this morning.

Where had that orange neon golf ball gone anyway? He hung over the side of the bed. Maybe it was underneath.

It wasn't.

Something else was there. Mixed in with the dust balls was a piece of crumpled-up paper. A note.

He lay back. How could he have forgotten?

He couldn't play golf today. He couldn't hang around and do nothing. He'd have to do something about that note . . . try to do something, anyway.

Outside there was a sound, a sharp high whistle.

It was J.P., the best whistler he had ever heard.

He didn't have time for J.P. now, not one minute.

He pulled up the screen and leaned out the window. "I have things to do. Important things."

J.P. squinted up, running her fingers through her inch-long red hair. "Forget about them."

The sun was so strong, Matthew could hardly see her turnipy face, with her freckled cheeks bulging out over a tiny pointed chin.

"Can't." He pulled in his head and reached for his sneakers . . . not the new ones with the terrific cushions. His mother had told him not to dare put a foot into them until school started.

He slid into the old ones, the ones with the holes in the toes. They were still wet from stamping in a puddle the hose had made yesterday.

J.P. whistled again—so loud, it rang in his ears.

He looked in the mirror. His mother had made him get a school haircut. It was disgusting. He could see a white line around the edges where his skin hadn't gotten tan.

He looked like some kind of idiot.

He yanked at the dresser drawer hard, almost

hard enough to pull the whole thing out, and grabbed a T-shirt.

J.P. was still whistling.

He slammed the drawer back in, smashing his finger.

"Yeow." He stuck his finger in his mouth, wanting to cry.

"What's the matter?" J.P. shouted up.

He took his finger out of his mouth, looking at the red mark on his nail. "Nothing," he yelled back irritably.

He looked at the red 1 on the wall again. "One finger almost cut off," he whispered.

He scooped up the note and went downstairs for breakfast.

Everyone had eaten already. His father had gone to work. His mother was in the basement with Laurie, painting the laundry room with the blue paint left over from his bedroom.

He could hear Laurie singing "Bunny Foo Foo," her favorite song. Every few minutes his mother would join in. She was having a great time painting everything. She had finished the kitchen last week. It was yellow now . . . "sun-flower gold," she had said. She had even painted a white flower over the sink.

His older sister, Cindy, had finished eating too. He knew because her toast crusts were scattered over the mat. She was probably up in her bedroom. All she did all day was try on clothes for school.

Matthew sat down at his place, and piled Honey Oats to the top of the bowl. He wouldn't look at the note he had found until he had finished.

It lay there in front of him, creased in about fourteen places. Laurie must have found it when she was drawing ones all over the place. Red lines marched across the *Dear Matthew* part.

He was in trouble. Lots of trouble.

He stared at the refrigerator. Crayon lines rolled along the bottom like red waves.

"Are you going to sit there forever?" a voice asked.

It was J.P. again.

He had forgotten all about her.

She was leaning against the door, her nose pressed against the screen, almost hanging into the kitchen.

"Just having my cereal," he said.

The milk was warm. He hated it warm.

It had always been warm in his old school, warm with little pieces of the container floating around on top.

If only he were going back to his own school, he wouldn't care about warm milk. He wouldn't have to worry about this note. He could just heave it into the garbage can.

J.P. opened the screen door and came inside. "What's the matter with you?"

He shook his head. "Nothing."

She slid onto a chair and helped herself to an animal cracker Laurie had left on the table.

"I see you have a note from Miss Bass," she said, mouth full.

Matthew raised one shoulder.

"Everybody gets one," she said. "It says you're supposed to read."

Matthew loaded more cereal onto his spoon. "I know that."

J.P. flicked her finger at the note. "Didn't do it?"

"Didn't have time."

J.P. reached for one of Cindy's crusts. "You had all summer. Days and days . . ."

"So I forgot."

"Miss Bass is a shark if you don't—" She started to laugh, spraying cracker crumbs. "Get it? Miss Bass, a shark?"

Matthew didn't laugh. He couldn't even smile. "I forgot about it," he said again.

J.P. chewed on the crust for a minute. "I have to tell you, Matthew," she said, looking serious, "Miss Bass loves to read. That's her favorite thing. Everyone knows that."

"Yes," Matthew said. His lips felt dry. Reading was his worst thing.

J.P. leaned forward. "Today might be your lucky day, Matthew. Today's the day I'm going to try to save your life."

2

"The library doesn't open until ten," J.P. said. "We can take the long way."

Matthew followed her along the curb. Everything in Deposit, Ohio, was different from his old neighborhood. The houses were skinnier and farther apart. There were more hills too.

It certainly seemed hotter. Right now his feet were heavy on the burning cement, and his toes stuck together inside his sneakers.

On Harding Avenue there wasn't a tree or a spot of shade in sight. Next to the dentist's office was a new store. They stopped in the doorway. A neon PETS—WE'RE OPEN sign flashed on and off over their heads.

Matthew leaned against the glass. Inside, the lights were dim. Everything was cool and green with birds chirping in leafy cages, and fish swimming around in bubbling tanks.

Fish. Shark. Bass. Matthew shook his head, trying not to think about Miss Bass.

He tried the door, rattling the knob.

Inside, a dog began to bark with a loud deep sound.

Matthew put his nose closer against the glass. To one side he could see a row of dogs behind silvery bars. They slept, stretched out on newspaper, all except for one, a black dog with long legs and gigantic paws.

He stopped barking when he saw Matthew staring at him, and tried to stand up in the cage.

A moment later he flopped back.

"He's too big for that cage, I think." Matthew kept watching the dog's eyes. They were large, and dark, and ". . . sad," he said aloud.

"I'd take him. Take him in one minute." J.P. leaned over Matthew's shoulder. "If only I didn't have a thousand allergies."

Matthew nodded. "Barney would hate it if I had a dog."

"He probably costs a million dollars anyway," J.P. said.

The dog was panting a little.

"I'd give him some water," Matthew said. "Food too. I'd—"

The dog stopped panting.

"It's almost as if he knows what you're saying," J.P. said.

The town clock began to chime. "Come on." She started to run.

Someone else was running too. A skinny boy with hair down in his eyes. He was wearing shorts, so Matthew could see he had scabs on both knees. The boy was racing toward the pet shop.

"Watch out," Matthew tried to tell J.P. "He's going to—"

Too late.

J.P. and the boy collided.

"Oof." J.P. staggered back. For a second she and the boy glared at each other. Then she turned her head. "Come on, Matthew. Let's go."

The library was a block away. It looked like the River Road School, long and low . . . but green leaves were growing up all over the sides and front. It was closed when they reached the door.

"Wouldn't you think people would open when they're supposed to?" J.P. asked over her shoulder.

Matthew watched her sink down on the steps. She began to whistle.

"Did you read . . ." he began. Maybe no one had read anything. Maybe no one paid attention. . . .

"Of course." She nodded, staring at him. "Don't worry, Matthew. You're going to be all right."

"It's okay for you to say that."

J.P. frowned. Her eyebrows came together like pale little caterpillars. "I have other things to worry about. You saw that kid. . . . You saw Frankie Corn. . . ."

Matthew saw that her green eyes seemed brighter than usual. Shiny. For a moment he wondered if she was going to cry.

He opened his mouth, but before he could ask her anything, she was whistling so loud, it rang in his ears.

He made believe he wasn't paying attention. Instead he reached into his pocket for the note and smoothed it out on his jeans. The writing was large, scrawled across the page. It was almost as bad as his own handwriting.

It had been signed by Barbara Bass, his new teacher. It said, at least he thought it said, that she was looking forward to having Matthew in her class.

It also said that she expected him to read a couple of books by the first day of school.

He tried to think about a book he might have read last year. He didn't even care if it was a good book. Now he'd be happy if he could think of any old book.

The only one he could think of was one of Laurie's. It was about a hen. The hen tried to get everyone to help her, but she finally had to do everything herself.

Laurie loved the clucking part at the end.

Matthew couldn't even remember the name of the book. Besides, it was a real baby thing. He'd die before he'd get up in front of the whole class and say he'd read that.

At last the shade in the library window snapped up.

"We're open," the man said. Mr. Cartucci? Mr. Cateechi? He had a huge yellow mustache. Mr. . . . ?

Matthew couldn't remember. He had been in the library only once since they moved to Deposit, Ohio, and he wasn't so hot with names anyway.

The mustache bristled when the man saw Matthew. He was probably thinking back to that other time when Matthew had been there. He was probably remembering that Matthew had come in for a drink, and dripped water all over his floor . . . water that had turned black when Matthew had tried to wipe it away with his sneakers.

J.P. sailed into the library ahead of Matthew. He followed her, listening to the sound of her rubber sandals slapping against the tiles. Rows of books stretched from the floor to the ceiling . . . millions of books. Matthew wondered if anyone had ever read all of them.

He hadn't even read one.

J.P. went back into a corner and pulled out a book. It was so heavy, she could hardly hold it.

"Here you are, Matthew. I'm going to save your life right now."

Matthew stared at the book. It was maroon. The edges had been dipped in gold. The man who made it must have been rich.

The book looked hard. Worse than hard. It looked impossible.

He sighed. "I can't read this."

"Neither can I." J.P. started to laugh. "The person who wrote it probably couldn't even read it."

Matthew gritted his teeth. He wanted to punch her right in her turnip face.

"See, Matthew? Things could be worse. That's what my grandmother always says."

She hefted the book back onto the shelf, then headed for the next room. CHILDREN'S SECTION, said the sign on the door.

Standing up on tiptoes, J.P. ran her fingers along the books. "Can you read?" she asked over her shoulder, and tipped one out.

"Of course I can read."

"Don't fool around with me, Matthew. Are you any good?"

"Uh . . . not . . ." Matthew looked at the book in her hand. He couldn't read it in a hundred years.

J.P. leaned forward. "Are you yuck-o?"

"No. What do you think . . ." His voice trailed off. J.P. would find out soon enough. He was worse than yuck-o. "Do they have special reading in the River Road School?" he asked.

J.P. shoved the book back on the shelf. "I was afraid of that."

She marched around to the other side of the stack. "How anyone can't read . . ."

He stuck out his lip. "I can read. It's just that I have a lot of other stuff to do. Better stuff."

J.P. grabbed four books off the shelf. "I'll keep you company. I'll read too."

She went over to Mr. Cartucci's desk, reaching into her pocket for her card.

It was filthy.

Matthew could see that the man with the mustache didn't even want to touch it. He picked it up with two fingers.

J.P. didn't notice, though. She was looking at Matthew. "Look," she said. "I don't want to spend every minute of my life reading, but even my grandmother says you have to read once in a while."

She picked up her card, folded it into her pocket, and took the books.

Matthew followed her out the door and down the street. He felt silly following a girl around.

He knew he was going to feel even sillier when J.P. found out how terrible a reader he really was. And the rest of the class too.

3

J.P.'s garage was cool, and shady, and smelled of paint. The sides were lined with shelves—shelves filled with boxes, and tools, and bunches of sticks nailed together. J.P.'s older brother, Warren, had started to build kites.

"Going into the kite-selling business," he had told Matthew last week. "Going to be rich by next March."

Right now Warren was off somewhere, playing ball probably. The car was gone too. "My father took it for a muffler or something," J.P. said, shrugging. "Good. Gives us plenty of room in here."

She pulled out an old piece of rug and covered a damp spot of oil on the cement floor. Then she plunked herself down. "By lunchtime you'll finish the first book, by the middle of the afternoon the second one. We'll get to the pool before it closes. . . ."

Matthew sank down on the edge of the rug and took the books she handed him.

They weren't very thick, but he couldn't read the titles of either one.

He sat there for a minute, turning them over.

"What's the matter?" she asked.

He shook his head.

She leaned over him. *"Shark!"*

"Sure, I knew that. I certainly—"

"And the other one is *Astronomy.*"

He raised his head quickly to be sure she wasn't making fun of him, but she looked serious, her caterpillar eyebrows drawn together. "Miss Bass will faint dead away when she hears you know such a big word."

She stopped for a breath. "As-tron-o-my. It's about stars."

He tried to say it after her.

"You have to practice it. If you don't know anything else, and you can just say—" She broke off. "My grandmother always says you have to put your best foot forward." J.P. nodded to herself. "And she's right, Matthew. Otherwise your whole year could be ruined."

He closed his eyes. J.P. was always going on about her grandmother. It was a good thing J.P.'s grandmother had moved to California and came for visits only once in a while. Matthew would hate to hear about her any more than he did already. The other day J.P. had told him she had won a prize for her brains.

He had told her his grandmother had won a prize too. He didn't say it was for guessing how many beans were in a bottle. He swallowed a little. He still missed his grandfather back in New York, back in his old neighborhood.

He opened the *Shark* book.

He knew about three words on the page.

"Don't worry if you don't know all the words," she said. "Look at the pictures. Look at the words you do know. Figure it out like a puzzle."

That would take him all day.

"And don't take all day," she said.

Matthew looked at the pictures. Sharks swimming across the page, mouths open, showing long, curved teeth.

He flipped to the middle. One shark took up both sides. " *'The great white,'* " he read slowly. " *'Hard to see because of its color. It sneaks up . . .'*"

Matthew shivered.

On the other side of the mat J.P. was turning pages quickly. A moment later she stood up. "The trouble with reading is it makes you hungry. Hungry for something salty. Be right back."

Matthew sat there staring at a picture of a dogfish shark. He thought back to this morning . . . the dog in the pet store. He had been a little ugly and sad.

A moment later J.P. slid under the garage doors with a pile of bags under her arms. "Potato chips. My favorite food."

"Barney's favorite too."

She grinned. "Some cat," she said, and tossed him a bag of Fig Newtons. "How's the book?"

Fig Newtons. They were his old reading teacher's favorite kind. He thought about telling J.P., but he remembered she didn't know about Mrs. Paris. She didn't know about his old school.

Matthew felt a tight feeling in his chest. He pictured Mrs. Paris getting ready for school tomorrow. Maybe she'd even be tucking Fig Newtons in her purse for her reading class.

"Matthew, are you listening to me? How's the book?" J.P. was asking.

Matthew tore open the top of the bag with his teeth.

"What's it about?"

"Sharks," he said.

J.P. sighed. "I know that."

He bit his lip. "I can't . . . Most of it is—"

J.P. looked over his shoulder. "My grandmother says you have to keep trying," she said, and began to read aloud. *"Dogfish,"* she began. She zipped through the page in two seconds flat. "Try the next one."

Matthew could feel the heat in his cheeks. He couldn't read the first word or the next one.

He wished he could stand up and get out of the garage. Fly out. He wished he never had to see her again. How could he be so stupid?

Suppose he did something like this in school? What would the rest of the kids think?

J.P. took the book out of his hand. She began to read. She read that page and the next and the one after that.

Her voice sounded good, except once in a while she'd stop for a potato chip, and the words would crunch up as she chewed.

Barney wandered in and sat on her lap. Now J.P. read between sneezes.

She was allergic to cats, Matthew remembered.

She didn't seem to mind, though.

By lunchtime the book was finished.

By three o'clock they had finished the second one. A real baby thing with "twinkle, twinkle, little star" on the first page.

So what.

As-tron-o-my sounded great.

It wasn't until later, much later, when he had climbed out of the pool and headed home for supper, that he remembered her saying, "I have other things to worry about." He thought about her eyes, green, shiny, almost teary.

He wondered what she had to worry about.

4

Matthew started down his front path. His mother had made him wear new jeans. They were stiff and scratchy.

He wondered if everyone was going to laugh at the way he looked.

Sure they would. He looked like a robot in pants that could stand up by themselves.

"Maa-fooo," a voice yelled from the window.

Matthew kept going, even though he could hardly bend his knees.

He took a quick look back at the house. It was different from his old house . . . but beginning to seem just right. The porch was filled with his mother's plants now, and his father had hung wind chimes that made tinkling sounds on a breezy day.

"Maa-fooo," Laurie yelled again.

He swiveled his head to see her in the window. His mother was at the window now, holding Laurie up. The screen was open and they were almost hanging out, waving.

Everyone in the town of Deposit, Ohio, could see them . . . his mother still in her bathrobe, and Laurie wearing nothing except her mermaid underpants.

Matthew looked around to see who was behind him. No one. Then he waved a little . . . a one-finger wave with his hand down next to his stiff scratchy jeans pocket.

"Good luck," his mother called.

"Good boy," Laurie said after her, thinking that was what she was trying to say.

Next door there was an explosion of sound.

Warren Peterson, J.P.'s older brother, burst out, the door slamming behind him. He raced down the street past Matthew, waving.

Warren was the biggest kid he knew. Big but

not fresh. J.P. was half his size and always fighting with him.

Right now she barreled out of her house. "I'm going to tear you apart, Warren," she was yelling. Then she saw Matthew, and slowed down. "Idiot brother," she said. "Took the last of the only cereal I like."

Behind Matthew, Laurie started to sing "Bunny Foo Foo" at the top of her lungs.

J.P. handed him a book. "Keep it under your arm," she said, talking loud over Laurie's voice. "Miss Bass will think you're a reader."

The book was a good size . . . not too fat, not too thin. There was a picture of a kid on the cover. His name was Homer.

Homer? He didn't know one kid in the world named Homer.

Homer was fooling around with a machine.

Matthew looked closer. Was it a doughnut machine? He tucked the book under his arm. Crazy to think of a kid making a doughnut machine.

He grinned a little, walking along the edge of the curb with J.P. Then he began to think about his old school, his old friends. The were probably walking to school at this same exact minute.

They didn't have to worry about a teacher who read all day long.

Up ahead he could see his older sister, Cindy. He knew she was worried about the new school too. He didn't know why she was worried. She always did everything she was supposed to do. Too bad she was wearing those false eyelashes again. Even his mother had told her they weren't a good idea.

J.P. had gotten a step or two ahead of him. She was hopping up and down the curb on one foot, whistling.

"What are you so happy about?" he asked, feeling angry.

J.P. looked up at him. She was the ugliest girl he had ever seen. Her turnip face was sunburned from the pool yesterday afternoon, and her red hair was cut so short, it looked as if she had hardly any. She was wearing . . . what was she wearing? Some kind of shorts and a top that was too big, or too puffy, or something.

She looked terrible, worse than he did.

"I am not happy." She leaned closer so he could see her forty or fifty freckles, her green eyes. "If you think I want to go back to school, to the worst kids in the universe . . ."

"The worst kids? What do you mean, worst?"

J.P. started to whistle again. She raised one shoulder in the air.

"What do you mean—" he began again.

"Just shut up about it, Matthew," she said, and began to run.

Matthew ran behind her. He could hear the swish-swish of his jeans, feel them against his thighs, stiff, hot, uncomfortable.

He didn't want to lose J.P. He didn't know where his class was, he didn't know what Miss Bass looked like . . . and then J.P. was gone too. It seemed she had disappeared into the bunches of kids in the school yard.

He turned in at the school-yard gates, taking a last look at Cindy, who was going another couple of blocks to the junior high. He hurried across the yard, trying to look as if he knew

where he was going. Kids were everywhere, running, yelling, playing ball. It seemed a lot noisier than the Polk Street school yard.

He wandered through a mess of mothers with little kids, a couple of them crying. Kindergarten.

Warren ran past. And then J.P., giving Warren a little punch on the arm before she darted off.

Matthew took a deep breath. He was so glad to see her, he almost felt like crying.

He followed her to the end of the school yard, trying to see which line she was looking for. He called to her, but the sound became part of the rest of the screaming going on all over the place.

Then he saw something else. Behind J.P. were two kids. Boys. No, three. There was a girl too.

They were walking the way she did, kind of holding their arms out, kind of hopping. One of them was the boy from yesterday, the skinny one in front of the pet store.

They looked tough. He wondered whether they'd make fun of him too.

Suddenly J.P. twirled around. She kicked out one leg.

The kids jumped back.

J.P.'s face was red, her mouth was open.

Matthew could see that her green eyes had tears in them. She didn't bother to brush them away. She just turned around again and kept going.

She stopped in a corner of the yard, and stood behind a ragged line. The room number 210 was painted in green on the cement. It was the only thing that was the same as his old school.

Matthew went over and stood in back of her. He tried to pretend he hadn't seen what just happened.

He ran his tongue over his lips. They felt dry, strange. "Where's the teacher?" he asked.

J.P. pointed.

A woman had opened the doors to the school. She was tall, huge, fierce-looking. She almost had to stoop to get through the door. She was carrying a pile of books. The pile of books was huge too. It reached as high as her chin.

"Told you, Matthew," J.P. said. "Told you she loves books."

Matthew swallowed. Quickly he opened the Homer book and tried to read the first page.

5

There was hardly any room in the classroom. Books were stacked everywhere. So were plants. A skeleton stood in one corner near a filthy-looking tan armchair. A sign over the chair said READING CORNER.

"Take a seat. Take a book," Miss Bass said. She waved her hand around. "Welcome."

Matthew ended up in a desk behind J.P. in the last row at the back of the room.

Next to him was the kid from the pet store, the kid who had collided with J.P. yesterday, the kid who had made fun of her behind her back this morning.

Reading
Corner

He was drawing—drawing on the cover of his notebook, and then on his new homework pad. He had already drawn a couple of fish on the backs of his hands.

He saw Matthew looking at him, and grinned. "I'm Frankie." He raised his T-shirt up a little. He had drawn an ear of corn on his stomach. "Frankie Corn."

"And what did you read this summer?" Miss Bass asked.

Matthew looked up. So did Frankie.

Frankie raised his shoulders in the air. "Uhm . . ."

Matthew could feel his own hands get wet. He was glad that J.P. had helped him with those books.

Frankie began to count on his fingers. "I read about fifteen books," he said, "maybe twenty. All about fish. Fighting fish. Neons. Setting up a saltwater tank. You know, like the ocean. . . ."

J.P. had turned around to look at Frankie. She was making faces.

Miss Bass was nodding. "Maybe we could

clean this place out a little. Make room for an aquarium."

She looked toward Matthew.

"More than one book," Matthew said quickly. He wasn't even sure Miss Bass was looking at him. "I'm working on this one now." He held up the Homer book.

"I can see you like to read," she said. "I like that one too. We'll have to talk about it."

Matthew was furious at himself. If only he had kept his mouth closed.

"Go on," said Miss Bass.

"Uh . . . what . . ."

"Summer books," she said.

Matthew looked at J.P. Her lips were drawn back, her teeth together. She was making *Sh* sounds. Shark.

He couldn't talk about that book. He'd sound almost as if he were copying Frankie Corn. "Astronomy," he said slowly, being sure to say it right. "That means stars and stuff."

"Yes," said Miss Bass.

Miss Bass was looking at him, looking hard. So was everyone else.

His hands felt wet.

He opened his mouth. He could see the first page, the words. "Twinkle, twinkle, little star . . ." he said.

Everyone laughed. Even Miss Bass.

Matthew looked down.

How could he have said that? How could he . . .

Then he realized. Everyone thought he was joking. Everyone thought he was a great reader, just fooling around with that twinkle twinkle stuff.

Wait until they found out the truth.

6

The second week of school was almost over. Right now it was "Grab a book and read" time.

It was always grab a book and read in Miss Bass's class. They didn't have regular reading the way they had in his last school. Everyone was reading a different book . . . and some kids were reading two.

The clock was inching its way toward three.

Matthew had just finished the Homer book J.P. had given him.

It was a riot of a book. Even though he couldn't read about half the words, it still made him laugh.

The book was covered with chocolate stains, probably from J.P.

Right now her face was turned toward the window. She was twirling her finger around the inch of hair she had on top of her head. She was chewing something too—chewing something with her mouth wide open.

Matthew shook his head. Frankie Corn was mean to J.P. But maybe that was because J.P. was always acting like an idiot.

He wished they got along better.

Frankie reminded him of his old friend Beast. Beast loved to draw too.

And they were both funny. Frankie had made him laugh so hard in the cafeteria today, he had spilt his milk all over the table.

They had nearly gotten into big trouble right after that. They had sneaked back into the room to get Frankie's baseball, even though it was a school rule to stay outside.

"Forget something?" Miss Bass always said. "Too bad. Think ahead."

They were rooting around in the closet, pushing each other, knocking things over, and a box teetered on the shelf, slipped before they could reach for it, and crashed on the floor.

"Christmas ornaments," Matthew had said.

"Not anymore," said Frankie, looking at the shattered pieces.

They could hear the classroom door open.

They stood still as statues as they heard Miss Bass come into the room.

"Anyone there?" she called.

Matthew put his hand over his mouth, wanting to laugh, even though he didn't feel like laughing one bit.

A moment later Miss Bass had gone.

They shoved the box of broken ornaments back on the shelf, and raced out the door.

"Forgot the baseball," Frankie had said.

"Too bad," Matthew had answered, his lips feeling stiff and strange. "Think ahead."

Right now Matthew shook his head. He wondered what would happen when Miss Bass opened her box of ornaments.

She was up in front with her head buried in a book, and next to him Frankie was drawing a fish on a piece of looseleaf. The middle hole at the edge of the paper was the fish's mouth.

Frankie drew a tic-tac-toe box on his paper, and leaned toward Matthew.

Matthew looked up at Miss Bass, then he put an X in the middle box.

"How about I come over to your house tomorrow," Frankie said. He drew an O with a face in the middle.

Matthew quickly put in another X. "Tomorrow?" He remembered that J.P. had said something about digging more golf holes in her lawn. "J.P. wants to—" he began.

Frankie ducked behind the kid in front of him so Miss Bass wouldn't see him talking. "Not J.P.," he whispered.

Matthew looked at the tic-tac-toe. "J.P. is—"

"J.P. is one big pain," Frankie said.

Miss Bass raised her head. "Finished your book, Matthew?"

He jumped.

"Come here for a minute."

Matthew slid out of his seat slowly and

walked toward the front of the room. He could feel his heart pounding, even though Miss Bass hadn't been near the closet.

Miss Bass's desk was filled with little piles of paper clips, and Band-Aids, and balls of string. There were pictures too. Pictures of kids, and dogs, a picture of an old man with a cane, and Miss Bass standing in front of a mountain. She looked almost as high as the mountain.

"Nothing to read?" Miss Bass asked.

Matthew tried to think of something to say. "I just finished my book. Going to start, ah . . . going to work on . . ." The truth was, he couldn't think of anything else to do. He didn't have another book.

Miss Bass reached into her bottom drawer. "Here's a book you'll love. It's about a boy and his younger brother. He's Peter, and the little one is Fudge."

Matthew tucked the book under his arm. He couldn't even look at her. Instead, he looked at the book she was reading. There was a picture of a dog on the page.

"That looks like the dog in the pet store," he said without thinking.

"A Labrador?"

"With sad eyes. Yes . . ." His voice trailed off.

"I love Labs," said Miss Bass. "They're big dogs, though, and they need lots of exercise." She pushed at her hair with one large hand. "One of these days I'm going to get myself a dog. A nice little dog that doesn't have to run around so much. Maybe a poodle."

In back, Frankie was staring at Matthew, his eyebrows raised as if he were asking a question.

Frankie was waiting for him to say he could come to Matthew's.

Matthew swallowed. He looked at J.P. At that moment she was pulling a strip of gum out of her mouth, looking cross-eyed at it.

J.P. was always doing the weirdest things.

Matthew nodded at Frankie. "Okay," he mouthed.

"How would you like to get out of here," Miss Bass was asking him. "That is, if you and Frankie are finished with your conversation."

"Out of here?" He took a quick look at her to see if she was joking.

Miss Bass went to the closet and opened the door. She reached into a red-and-yellow-striped bag and pulled out a set of keys.

"Will you"—she went back to her desk and reached underneath—"put this in my car?"

She handed him a knobby brown paper package.

Matthew reached for it. He could see that underneath Miss Bass's desk was a mess of stuff. Shopping bags, pieces of chalk, and old magazines were piled on top of each other. He wondered where she put her feet when she sat down.

"Matthew, wake up. Take this bag to my car." Miss Bass dangled the key in front of him.

Matthew took the bag and the key, and wandered out the door. He went as slowly as he could to take more time.

He ran the key lightly along the wall, thinking about the dog. He wondered if he ever got out

of the cage, if he ever got to walk around, or run.

It was too bad Barney, his cat, didn't like dogs. Barney was terrified of dogs. Last night she had heard one bark on TV. She streaked upstairs and hid under the bed for an hour.

Matthew thought about J.P. What was he going to tell her about tomorrow?

"Matthew," a voice boomed from behind him.

Matthew whirled around.

Miss Bass was leaning out the classroom door. "Do you know which one my car is?"

"No, I guess—"

"It's the green one," Miss Bass said. "The little green—"

"That's yours?" It was a great car. Sporty. The kind he was going to have if he ever got rich.

"That's mine," she said.

Matthew nodded his head once or twice.

"Don't scratch the wall," she said.

"Scratch . . ." Matthew repeated. What was she talking about?

"The key . . . dragging it along the wall."

"Yes," Matthew said. "I mean no."

He hurried down the hall and out the door.

It was warm outside, the sun shining down, a perfect day for the pool. Too bad the pool was closed now. He and J.P. had climbed halfway up the fence to look at it yesterday. There was a cover on top, thick and tight.

He didn't like to look at it like that, all ready for winter. He liked to think about it with the clear water shimmering in the sun. He liked to think about J.P. swimming across it, her arms pumping, her legs kicking up an explosion of waves in back of her. In school J.P. was different, terrible. All she did was make faces, or hop around. And all she talked about was her grandmother.

Matthew crossed the parking lot, looking for Miss Bass's little green car. It was at the very end. The license plate read SHARK.

Matthew turned the key in the lock. The door swung open under his hand, and the air, hot as a blister, rushed out. He took a breath, shoved the key in his pocket, and put the package on the seat.

It was so hot, he wondered how Miss Bass would ever sit on it. He grinned to himself thinking about her flying off the seat through the roof of the car.

He pressed the lock down, and slammed the car door back on the heat.

Inside the school, the bell rang. It was finally time to go home.

Matthew wondered if he was supposed to go back to the classroom. That would be pretty silly, he thought. He'd just about get there and have to turn around and march out the door again.

He took a breath. He was glad to be out, glad to forget about the Christmas ornaments until Monday morning.

He walked out the gate slowly, then started to run. Maybe he'd pass the pet store. He'd take a quick look. The dog had probably been sold by now anyway.

Good . . . then he could forget about the whole thing.

7

Matthew ran all the way home from the pet store. He ran until he had a stitch in his side and could hardly take a breath.

The dog hadn't been in the same cage today, hadn't been in any of the cages. Matthew had wandered up and down the aisles looking for him.

In back a man was combing a fat tan cat. His hair was the same color as the cat. It hung down in a ponytail that was tied with a brown shoelace.

Even his shirt was tan. In large letters across the front it said: DID YOU SQUEEZE YOUR PET TO-

DAY? Underneath was a picture of a snake wrapped around a man.

Matthew cleared his throat. "You know that dog you have?"

"The cute one? Sold."

"Who . . ."

"Father, mother, couple of kids. Nice dog, nice kids."

Matthew nodded, then went back down the aisle again. He felt a tightness in his chest begin to loosen. It was nice to think about Blackie running around someone's backyard.

Then he heard the barking, Blackie's deep loud bark.

He turned. The dog was in a cage in the corner. "I thought you told me . . ." he said to the man.

"That dog? You mean that one? I thought you meant the little white one. No one wants a big one like that . . . one who barks all the time . . . needs to run around the world at least once a day. . . . I don't even know why I hold on to him."

Matthew walked toward the dog slowly. "I

54

have to get home," he told the man over his shoulder. "Have to . . ."

"Great dog for a kid like you."

"I don't have any money," Matthew said. "Only a dollar I found."

"The dog is free," the man said. "You just have to pay for the collar."

The dog stopped barking. He half stood in his cage. His dark eyes watched Matthew.

Matthew reached out. He poked a finger into the cage. He felt the dog's smooth coat, his soft tongue. "I have a cat," he said.

Behind him the man was shoveling out the food, not paying attention anymore, humming a little.

Matthew started down the aisle, listening to the dog begin to bark again. He hurried, not wanting to hear the sound of it.

A moment later he was out the door, running.

He cut across his lawn, then looked up the driveway. Laurie's toys were strewn all over the place: her fire truck, about forty red and yellow blocks, a bashed-in tea set, and her doll, Patty Cake.

Something was wrong with Patty Cake. Her inside strings had loosened so her head was held on by one long cord. Sometimes when Laurie walked along holding her, Patty Cake's head bumped down on the sidewalk in back of her.

Ahead of him Matthew could see his cat, Barney, wandering into J.P.'s garage. He stepped over Laurie's Go-Go lawn mower, and started after her.

Warren had two kites hanging on hooks now. One was red with strips of blue fringe, and the other had a monster face.

J.P. was crouched in the middle of the floor, bending over, drawing something on one of Warren's half-finished kites.

Matthew wondered if she'd ruin it. J.P. always had to mess things up.

He watched her for a second. She looked sad. She didn't even seem to notice that Barney had walked in and was rubbing her head against J.P.'s feet.

Something was wrong, but Matthew didn't have to wonder about it. He knew. J.P. was what was wrong. She couldn't get along with Frankie Corn. She couldn't get along with the other kids. She made faces. She . . .

He wanted to turn around and go back, but he couldn't do that. J.P. would hear him if he took a step.

Her hair had grown a tiny bit around the edges, he noticed. It didn't make any difference, though, she'd probably just chop it off again.

He rocked back and forth on his new Jetstream sneakers, heel to toe, toe to heel, trying to decide what to do, what to say.

J.P. sneezed a little as Barney curled herself into a small gray-striped ball next to the kite.

Behind them was a loud knocking sound.

Before Matthew could turn around, J.P. jumped up and saw him. She dived toward him, grabbing his arm, and pulled him into the garage.

"What—" he began.

"Shhh," she whispered. "Don't talk. Don't even breathe."

The knocking came again.

J.P. pointed over Matthew's shoulder.

For a moment he couldn't move. Then he spun around.

Someone was standing on the side steps of his house, next to the driveway.

From where he was standing, the bushes were in the way. The person was so tall, though, it could only be Miss Bass.

Next to him J.P. stood up on tiptoes, frowning, her eyebrows pulled together.

Silently, they went to the end of the garage, and dived behind the side of the wall. Matthew could see Miss Bass's sneakers, huge white ones.

For one quick moment he raised his head up over the bushes. Just before J.P. pulled him down again, he saw it really was Miss Bass. She was frowning.

Of course, Miss Bass didn't know the bell didn't ring. His mother hadn't gotten around to fixing that yet.

Crouched next to him, J.P. asked, "What did you do?" Her lips barely moved.

Matthew raised one shoulder in the air. He could see the box of ornaments teetering on the edge of the shelf.

He drew in his breath. Somehow Miss Bass must have found out about it. Somehow she must have known they were hiding in the closet, not answering. And worse, she had probably opened the box of ornaments, seen . . .

He wondered what she was going to do. Tell his mother? Say that he was expelled?

He could feel his heart beating, pounding, could feel his face hot and red.

Suppose his mother looked out the window.

Suppose Cindy came home from school at that very minute . . . turned up the drive-way . . .

Next to him J.P. was standing like a statue. "Don't worry," she said.

After a long time Miss Bass went back down the steps, and along the grassy part of the drive-way to the street.

A moment later they couldn't see her any-more.

Matthew looked at J.P.

"Maybe it's nothing," she said. "Maybe . . ."

He didn't answer. He didn't want to talk, didn't even want to think.

Barney circled around him, looking up at his face.

Barney was a good cat, Matthew thought, a smart cat. She knew he was probably in the worst trouble of his life.

"I have another book for you to read," J.P. said.

"Uh . . . no, thanks. I—"

"Matthew, it's the saddest book you ever read in your life. About a boy who dies. He gets bitten by a . . . No, I won't tell you. You have to . . ."

She went through her books. "Here."

Matthew took the book. It was easier than arguing. Then he picked Barney up, and went along the driveway to the side door of his house.

J.P. called after him. "Don't forget about golf tomorrow. We want to dig about a hundred more holes."

Matthew fumbled with the door. "I'm not sure . . . I'm not . . ."

"What?"

The door opened. He slid inside.

8

It was Saturday morning.

Matthew turned the page of J.P.'s book. There were a lot of words he couldn't read. But one thing he knew.

The book was sad—so sad, he felt like crying. The boy's best friend had just died.

Matthew stared up at the red 1 on the wall. Having your best friend die was a lot worse than being in trouble with your teacher. He couldn't stop feeling scared, though. He wondered what would happen when he got to school on Monday.

Matthew thought about the boy in the book. He wondered what he would have done.

He didn't have to wonder. He would have gone to the teacher on Monday, told her the truth.

Matthew sighed, then he glanced at the clock on his dresser. Four-thirty, it said.

It always said four-thirty. Something was wrong with the hands. It had a nice loud ticking sound, though, a friendly sound.

The sun was strong through the window. It must be ten o'clock at least. Any minute J.P. would be standing in the driveway calling him.

He tried to decide what he was going to do. Maybe he could tell her he was going to work on his "My Pet" story.

That was really true. He had done only two sentences so far. They were pretty good, though. He had even used talking the way Miss Bass had taught them: *"MEOW," went Barney. She was a ferce cat.*

Matthew stood up and went to his window. Outside Warren was kneeling in his driveway, working on another kite. J.P. was playing golf by herself in her yard.

She was probably waiting for him.

For a moment he watched her. Every time she sank the ball into one of the holes they had dug this summer, she jumped up and down as if she were playing a real game.

Her feet didn't land at the same time, and her arms flew around as if they didn't belong together. And as soon as she stopped jumping up and down, she looked quiet, with her mouth turned down a little.

From the corner of his window Matthew could see across the driveway and down the street. He angled his head to see if Frankie Corn was coming.

Someone was walking along the street, but it was too far to see who it was.

Next door, J.P. was swinging her golf club around on the lawn. Tiny pieces of grass shot up in back of her. He wished she'd go inside.

Suppose she saw Frankie? Suppose she saw him coming up Matthew's path, heard him calling him? Maybe she'd come around to the front to ask what they were doing. Maybe she'd want to hang out with them too.

And Frankie would say . . .

Matthew took a deep breath. Frankie would say, "Get lost."

Matthew watched J.P. She looked so silly out there, so dumb.

She'd hate it that he had another friend.

He looked down the street again. It was Frankie Corn. He was coming along fast.

In about a minute he'd be in front of Matthew's house.

J.P. was at the last golf hole now.

Maybe she'd go inside in another minute.

Frankie Corn was six houses away.

"Hurry," Matthew whispered to J.P. He looked at the red 1 on his wall. One more golf hole.

The ball went in. J.P. jumped up and down.

Now, he told himself. *Go into the house. Do your homework. Turn on the TV. Do something.*

What she did was go back to the first golf hole and start over again.

Frankie was three houses away. Somehow Matthew had to get him out of there before J.P. looked up the driveway and saw them.

Matthew took the stairs two at a time, down to the second floor, down to the first, and out the door. He looked over his shoulder. From where he was, J.P. couldn't see him.

Maybe she couldn't see Frankie either.

Matthew was across his lawn, dashing past the front of J.P.'s house, when Frankie spotted him. "Hey, Matthew."

Matthew held up his hand. "Shhh." He grabbed Frankie's arm. "Hurry. Let's go."

Frankie stopped in front of the driveway. "What?"

"Just keep going," Matthew whispered.

Frankie started up again, slowly. "What's the matter? Where are we going?"

"Anywhere. Anywhere you want." Matthew tried to walk as fast as he could, without making noise.

If they could get to the corner, cross the street . . .

By the time they reached the last house, Matthew looked back. J.P. was standing there, watching him. She reached up and smoothed her hair.

Matthew turned around again quickly, barely listening as Frankie talked about going over to the pet store, and the catfish he was going to buy for his tank.

All the way to the avenue Matthew could see J.P. in his mind. J.P. with the golf club in her hand, standing there, and not even calling out to him.

What else could go wrong?

He turned to Frankie. "Did Miss Bass come to your house yesterday?"

Frankie raised one shoulder in the air. "Why would she do that?"

"The box of—"

"Don't think about that now," Frankie said. "Don't think about getting expelled."

"Do you think—" Matthew began.

Frankie looked serious, worried. "I think we're in big trouble."

9

Matthew took a deep breath. The pet store had an odd smell this morning.

"Hamster food," Frankie said, wrinkling his nose.

While Frankie headed toward the back of the store, Matthew wandered down one of the aisles. He wasn't going to go near the back today. He wasn't even going to see that dog.

He spotted a new aquarium with a sign in front. SALTWATER TANK—SHARKS.

They were small sharks, though, only about as long as his hand. He watched a few of them gliding along together. He remembered reading about fish traveling in schools.

School. He sighed, thinking about J.P. He wondered why she hadn't called after him, hadn't said, "Wait up, Matthew," hadn't said, "What about golf?"

Next to the turtles was a tank of neons. The small blue-and-red-striped fish streaked from one end to the other, back and forth, at a dizzying speed.

In Matthew's class in his old school there had been a tank with two fish on the science table. Harry and . . . he couldn't remember the name of the other one. It was a mean fish, always diving in front of Harry, grabbing all the food.

Matthew stood at the end of the aisle, frowning.

How could he have forgotten that fish's name?

Maybe soon he wouldn't remember anything about his old school.

Drake. The fish's name was Drake.

See? Nothing to it.

"Matthew?" Frankie called.

"Where are you?" Matthew called back.

The dog began to bark.

Matthew hurried up the aisle toward Frankie, pretending he didn't hear the noise of it.

"Look at this guy." Frankie pointed to a fish on the bottom of a tank.

Its mouth was open in a round O. It looked as if it were glued to the glass.

It was the ugliest thing Matthew had ever seen.

"Catfish," said Frankie. "Terrific, isn't it? Like one of those dinosaurs, you know, not the big one. The smaller one with the hump on its back."

Matthew nodded. He didn't know one thing about dinosaurs. He watched the catfish swing along the bottom of the tank, sucking at the glass.

"He's taking all the algae and stuff," Frankie said. "Cleaning the whole tank."

In back Blackie was still barking. His voice was beginning to sound hoarse.

Matthew thought about rubbing his hand along the dog's smooth coat, running home, asking his mother . . .

"I think I'll write the 'My Pet' story about this one," Frankie said.

"The dog?"

"Are you crazy? The catfish."

Before Matthew could answer, Frankie jumped him, arms around his neck. "Fight for your life," he yelled.

He sounded like Beast.

Matthew twisted around. He grabbed Frankie's waist. "Worm head," he yelled.

By this time all the dogs were barking.

Matthew started to laugh. He could feel things dropping out of his pocket, a penny rolling around, the clink of something else, a button from his shirt.

The pet store man grabbed them. "You two want a lesson in karate?"

Matthew looked up at him. The man was laughing too. Today he was wearing a green shirt, a shirt that said PET ME LIGHTLY. Underneath was a picture of an alligator with its mouth open.

Frankie spun free. He began to crawl around

the floor under the tanks, gathering up the stuff they had dropped. "Going to get that catfish," he yelled to the man over the noise of the dogs.

They waited while the man used a net to poke around in the tank.

It took him about five minutes to get the fish into the net and pop it into a plastic bag filled with water. "You make me work for my money," he told them.

He glanced over at Matthew. "That dog likes you," he said. "Cried after you for about a half hour last night."

Matthew swallowed.

"Too bad he's so big." The man wiped his hands on his shirt.

Matthew looked toward the corner of the store. He'd have to go farther down the aisle if he wanted to see the dog, see Blackie.

He didn't want to see him. He felt himself moving, though, going toward the corner, toward the cage.

The dog was waiting, wagging his tail furiously.

"I can't," Matthew told him. "My mother and

father . . . even if they said yes . . . what about Barn—"

In back Frankie was counting out the money, talking with the man.

Matthew could hear the bells on the town clock chiming. Noon. He poked his finger into the cage, feeling the dog's cold nose, his warm tongue.

"Come on, Frankie," he said after a minute. "I'm supposed to be home by lunch."

He walked backward away from the cage, trying not to look at the dog's eyes. They were so large, so dark, so sad-looking.

He met Frankie at the front of the store.

"No fooling around now," Frankie said. "I've got to get this beauty home without breaking the bag."

Behind them the pet store door opened again. The man leaned out. He was dangling a set of keys from his fingers. "One of you lose these?"

"Nah," Frankie said.

Matthew opened his mouth. He had seen the keys before. "Wait . . ." He closed his eyes. He could see Miss Bass . . . Miss Bass handing him the car keys in the classroom. Miss Bass's finger on his doorbell.

Matthew held out his hand. "Mine," he said as he took the keys. "At least . . ." His voice trailed off.

He wondered how Miss Bass had gotten home yesterday.

10

On Sunday, Matthew was stretched out across his bed, with J.P.'s book in front of him.

He read the last page and sat up. Ridiculous to cry over a book, he thought. He'd never tell anyone he had tears in his eyes.

He looked over at the red 1 on the wall.

Everything was wrong.

He slid off the bed and went downstairs for breakfast.

His father was making omelets.

They were the worst, all egg-runny with chunks of ham sticking up.

Laurie hated them too. She was sitting in her high chair, her lips closed tight. She was shaking her head no, as his mother tried to spoon omelet into her mouth.

"Hey, Maffoo," she said when she saw him.

His mother shoved in a lump of egg.

"Not good." Laurie sputtered.

Matthew laughed. He didn't feel like laughing, though. He was sick of worrying about everything.

Cindy was sitting on the countertop, swinging her legs back and forth. "I'm sick of worrying about everything," she said.

Matthew grunted. "What do you have to worry about?" He grabbed two pieces of bread and began to spread peanut butter on them. He hardly listened as she talked about some silly social studies homework.

As soon as she stopped for a breath, Matthew began to talk. "Suppose there was this dog?" he asked. "A dog who needed a home."

Cindy blinked. "What does a dog have to do with the Amazon River?"

"Nothing." Matthew opened his mouth wide at Laurie.

She was too smart, though. She kept her mouth in a thin little line against the next spoonful of egg.

"We're talking about my social studies assignment," Cindy said. "Not some dumb dog."

"Smarter than you," said Matthew.

"What dog?" his mother asked.

"Can a cat get along with a dog?" Matthew asked.

"What cat?" said his mother.

"The Amazon River," Cindy said. "I have to do a whole page—"

"Our cat," Matthew said.

"It would take a lot of effort," his mother said. "You'd really have to work at it."

"I wouldn't mind . . ." Matthew began.

His mother looked at him, shaking her head. "I would. I have enough to do around here without refereeing cat-and-dog fights."

"But . . ." Matthew looked at his mother's face. She had that look. The answer was no. She'd never take the dog.

He felt a lump in his throat and in his chest. He shoved the peanut butter sandwich into the garbage bag when his mother wasn't looking.

J.P.'s grandmother would have said he should eat it for the starving children who didn't have peanut butter.

He felt as if he wouldn't ever be able to swallow anything.

He went down the driveway, trying to decide what to do next. He angled his head to see into J.P.'s backyard. He wondered what she was doing. He hadn't seen her since yesterday morning, hadn't heard her yelling, or whistling.

He sighed. He thought about ringing her bell, asking her to come out and play golf, pretend that he had forgotten about yesterday.

He couldn't do that.

Maybe he'd walk over to the school yard, see if Miss Bass's car was still there.

It was getting cool, much cooler than it had been last week. If he could only rewind this whole week. He would have gone back to the classroom with the keys. He would have told

Frankie he had to dig golf holes with J.P. He could have said J.P.'s not so bad. He could have . . .

Someone was behind him.

J.P.

For a moment he didn't say anything, but it was too quiet.

"I have Miss Bass's car keys," he said.

J.P.'s mouth opened. "That's why she was—"

"—looking for me Friday."

It was quiet again. He thought about telling her about the ornaments, but he didn't want to talk about Frankie Corn.

"I worked on my cat story last night," he said.

"I worked on mine too," said J.P. "Stegosaurus."

Matthew frowned. He had heard that word before. He just couldn't . . .

"You know," she said. "The dinosaur."

"Your pet is going to be a dinosaur?" he asked.

He could just imagine Frankie Corn laughing. He could imagine everyone laughing.

"I told how he roamed the earth, stuff like that."

Matthew looked at her sideways. She started to whistle, hopping on one foot.

Two kids were going by on bicycles. They turned around to look at her.

"Will you stop that hopping," he exploded before he could think. "No wonder no one wants you around."

His mouth was suddenly dry.

J.P. was standing at the edge of the driveway, standing still, her hair poking up a little. Her face looked strange, her teeth biting down on her lower lip.

He started down the street and turned back. "Want to go over to the school yard?"

He began to run. "Come on," he said over his shoulder.

He knew she wasn't coming, though. He knew she was still standing there in the same spot, watching him.

11

Matthew walked across the school yard, thinking about J.P.'s face, her hair sticking up, her green eyes surprised.

Then he saw Miss Bass at the other end of the yard. She wasn't trying to open her car. She was playing basketball—playing by herself. First she raced down the yard, bouncing the ball against the pavement, then shot up at the hoop.

She missed every time.

He walked toward her slowly, wishing he could run away somewhere, keep running and never come back.

She saw him, and shot the ball at him. "Great work, Matthew," she said as he missed.

"I'm not too good at—"

"Ball, or remembering keys?"

"I'm sorry," he said. "I'm really—"

"Some friend you are," she said.

"I didn't think about—"

"Thinking's important," she said, but she was smiling a little.

"I guess so."

"You had my house key too."

"You had to stay in the school yard all weekend?" Matthew asked, hardly able to swallow.

"Oh, Matthew." She laughed. "No. I just live two blocks away. I walked over there, broke a window, and climbed in like a burglar."

Matthew nodded a little, picturing Miss Bass being able to squeeze through a window.

He wondered if J.P. was still standing in the driveway. They'd never be friends again now.

"Usually I don't take the car," Miss Bass was saying, "but someone had given me a bag of peaches . . ."

One thing, he'd never have to hear about J.P.'s grandmother again.

"I live alone," said Miss Bass, "and there were so many peaches. I thought I'd stew them up for the class."

He'd probably miss J.P.'s grandmother.

He'd miss J.P.

Miss Bass leaned forward. "So you forgot to give me the keys, Matthew. It's not the end of the world."

"I went back into the classroom at lunchtime. I dropped your box of ornaments. They crashed. . . ."

Miss Bass shook her head. "Isn't it the oddest thing, Matt? You do something wrong, and then something else happens, and something else, and it ends up in the biggest mess."

She bounced the ball. "I learned that the hard way too. Now I try to stick to the rules."

"I'm going to—" he began.

"I think you will too," she said. "It's all right. We'll have to decorate the tree with something else."

Matthew looked down at his sneakers. Miss Bass had to be the greatest teacher he knew.

And then he saw J.P. She was down at the end of Marita Street, walking slowly, going away from them. She wasn't hopping the way she usually did. Her shoulders were slumped and—

"What is it, Matthew?" Miss Bass asked.

"Nothing." His lips weren't right, though. They wouldn't stay straight. "There's a dog stuck in a cage. . . ."

"Terrible," said Miss Bass. "It's like that book—"

"I can't read either," Matthew said.

Miss Bass snorted. "You have your head stuck in a book all day. You read like a shark."

J.P. had disappeared around the corner. He looked back at Miss Bass. And then he thought about what she had said. His nose in a book. Reading. Every spare minute. It was true. "I love to read," he said.

He was so surprised, he said it again. "I love to read."

And he knew it was true. He didn't think about reading the words on the pages anymore. Somehow, they had turned into stories . . .

stories about a boy with a doughnut machine, and a little kid eating a turtle, and a boy's best friend who had died because of a bee sting.

And he thought about all the books in the classroom, and then the ones in the library. And he thought about reading all those books every day forever.

And he knew he had to tell J.P. right away.

"Where are you going?" Miss Bass said.

"I have to . . ." Matthew began. Even though J.P. would never be friends with him again, he had to tell her. Tell her that he'd never have to worry about not being a reader anymore. Tell her that it was all because of her. Tell her that her grandmother was right, that you just had to keep trying.

He was halfway across the school yard, heading for the gate.

"How about the keys?" Miss Bass was calling after him.

Matthew fumbled in his pocket. He opened his mouth.

"I can't believe it," she said. "You left them somewhere."

"Home." He raced out of the school yard. "I'll bring them right—"

"Don't worry," she said. "It's . . ."

He didn't hear the end of it. He was tearing up the block toward Marita Street.

12

Matthew spotted J.P. on the far corner, near the curb, her arms around the fattest tree on the block.

Her hair was poked up and her arms were a mess of scabs.

She was looking up through the thick green leaves at a squirrel, or a bird.

He thought about the books she had given him, and how neat she was with Barney.

Even her face looked better somehow, softer.

He stood there watching her for a moment without her seeing him.

Then a small brown acorn dropped out of the tree, and she jumped.

"Matthew?" she said as she turned toward him.

He took a step and opened his mouth. "Listen, J.P."

"There's a squirrel up there," she said, pointing to the branches. "He's tossing stuff at me."

"You're my best friend," he said. He thought about Beast, his best friend in his old neighborhood, his old school. But Beast would understand.

J.P. leaned back against the tree, and slid down until she was sitting underneath. "I never had a best friend before," she said.

He opened his mouth to tell her he was sorry about what he had said. But before he could say a word, she leaned forward. "Miss Bass told me," she said, "that she was taller than anyone in her class."

J.P. looked up as a pair of leaves floated down from the tree. "Miss Bass said she was a beanpole, a mess, and she couldn't get along with one person."

"Miss Bass?"

J.P. picked up the leaves and held them up to

the light. "This summer. I helped her get the classroom ready. She told me she found out you have to practice being a friend."

Matthew watched J.P. turning the leaves. She was staring at them, her green eyes filled with tears.

"I know I'm a mess too." Her voice was so low, he could hardly hear her. "Miss Bass said why didn't I practice on you? She said you'd make a great friend."

"Me?"

J.P. put the leaves in her lap. She looked up at the tree. "You're right about my hopping around," she said. "I don't know why I do stuff like that."

Matthew shook his head. "I'm sorry. I'm really—"

"You're wrong about the stegosaurus thing, though. It's fun to say you have a dinosaur for a pet."

Matthew thought about it. She was right. It was really funny when he thought about it. "About the reading . . ." he began. "If it wasn't for you, I would never have read."

He leaned forward. "You know that sad book? I even—"

"Cried," J.P. finished for him. "Everyone cries at that book. My grandmother . . ."

Her grandmother. Matthew took a deep breath. He wanted to say, *Do you always have to talk about your grandmother? Do you always—*

"My grandmother taught me to read." J.P. stopped and began again. "You know what? She said I was beautiful inside."

She raised her head. "She said if you're beautiful inside, it'll come on the outside someday."

An acorn popped out of the tree and bounced off her head.

They both laughed. But suddenly Matthew knew that J.P.'s grandmother was right again. And then he thought about Miss Bass. He could almost picture how the kids might have laughed at her.

And the dog. Too big, too loud . . .

He drew in his breath. "J.P.," he said, "I have an idea. I have the greatest idea you ever heard in your life."

"About dinosaurs?"

He blinked. "What are you talking about? No, of course not."

He heard the town clock chiming. It would be five o'clock in fifteen minutes.

He told her what he was thinking as fast as he could, the words tumbling out.

She scrambled to her feet, brushing shreds of leaves off her jeans and out of her hair.

"Hurry," he yelled.

Then they tore down the street toward home.

13

It was almost five o'clock. Matthew was out of breath. He had a stitch in his side. And he couldn't find that dollar, couldn't find it anywhere. He poked his head under the bed, looked under the dresser, and felt around on the closet floor.

Maybe in his dresser.

Too bad. There wasn't time.

J.P. was outside, whistling at the top of her lungs.

"It's two minutes to five," she screeched.

Matthew raced down the stairs again and out the door. He stopped short.

A kite was flying above J.P. and Warren's garage. It was orange with bright green letters. The letters were big and a little straggly:

WARREN'S KITES FOR SALE
WORLD'S GREATEST BROTHER

"I did this before." J.P. waved her hand. "I'm practicing being a good sister too," she said. "I can't wait to see what he says when he gets home from playing ball."

Then they took off running.

"We'll never make it," he said.

"We have to make it," J.P. said. "My grandmother always says . . ." She didn't have enough breath to finish.

They arrived at the pet store just as the man was locking up.

"The dog—" Matthew began.

"We don't have money for a collar—" J.P. cut in.

"Tomorrow," said Matthew. "I have a dollar somewhere. I just . . ."

The man smiled. "That's the least of my worries. But what about your cat?"

Matthew shook his head. "It won't be—"

J.P. shook hers too. "It's—"

"As long as you worked everything out," the man said.

All the time they were walking toward the cage, and the dog was barking, listening to them as they came.

When the man opened the cage door, the dog sprang out, standing high enough to put his front paws on Matthew's shoulders, and to lick J.P.'s turnipy face.

"Hey, Blackie," Matthew said.

J.P. shook her head. "It's not going to be your dog, Matthew. My grandmother always says a person should name his own dog."

The man snapped a red collar around the dog's neck, and handed Matthew the other end of the leash. "You're on your way," he said.

"Do you know where we're going?" J.P. asked Matthew.

He thought for a moment. "Not exactly."

J.P. grinned. "It's a good thing I do."

Matthew grinned back. "Is that what your grandmother always says?"

He followed her out the door, calling back to the man, "Thanks for the collar."

Then he started to run, holding the dog's leash, trying to keep up with both of them.

A few minutes later they stopped in front of a small brick house. It was covered with ivy—but not so much ivy that Matthew couldn't see that one of the windows was broken.

At that moment Miss Bass came around the side of the house.

It was almost as if the dog knew he was home. He raced toward her, pulling the leash out of Matthew's hand.

Miss Bass knelt down in time to put her big arms around the dog as he ran his tongue over her face, whining softly.

She looked up at Matthew and J.P. "Say this dog hasn't got a home. Say he belongs to me."

Matthew felt a smile coming on his face. He thought he had never felt so happy. "We're going to walk him for you," he said.

"Every day," said J.P.

"How did I ever think I wanted a tiny dog?" said Miss Bass. She was sitting on the ground now, the dog half in her lap. "I think I'll call him Thanksgiving."

"Better name than Blackie," said J.P.

Matthew nodded, still smiling.

Mrs. Bass smiled back. "How about my keys, Matthew?"

His mouth opened. "I . . ."

"I have another book for you," Miss Bass said. "It's about a boy who never remembers. He's a great kid, though—a great kid."

Miss Bass went inside with Thanksgiving to get the book.

Matthew could hear the town clock chiming again. It was time for dinner. Then right after that he'd start to read. Now he had two books to do, just like some of the other kids.

He couldn't wait to begin.

About the Author

Patricia Reilly Giff is the author of over fifty books for young readers, including the Kids of the Polk Street School books, the New Kids at the Polk Street School books, and the Polka Dot Private Eye books. A former teacher and reading consultant, she received her bachelor's degree from Marymount College and a master's degree from St. John's. She holds a Professional Diploma in Reading and a Doctorate of Humane Letters from Hofstra University.

Mrs. Giff lives in Weston, Connecticut.

About the Illustrator

Blanche Sims has illustrated all Patricia Reilly Giff's Polk Street School books. She lives in Westport, Connecticut.